THE
MAGNANIMOUS
Penny
CAMPAIGN

(The Coco Series)

THE
MAGNANIMOUS
Penny
CAMPAIGN

(The Coco Series)

Sheryl Tillis

XULON PRESS

Xulon Press
2301 Lucien Way #415
Maitland, FL 32751
407.339.4217
www.xulonpress.com

Paperback ISBN-13: 978-1-66282-718-1
Ebook ISBN-13: 978-1-66282-719-8

DEDICATION

To those who have a love for helping others;
your good deeds shall be rewarded.

Give and it shall be given unto you; good
measure, pressed down and shaken together, and
running over, shall men give unto your bosom.
Luke 6:38 KJV

ACKNOWLEDGEMENTS

The cover of *The Magnanimous Penny Campaign* is illustrated by Leslie Rowlands, a Tulsa native, Choctaw artist with over twenty eight years of experience working in fine arts. Leslie has a BFA degree from OSU. She also has a diverse career traversing as a freelance artist, interior artist, and decorative artist. Leslie is currently an art educator. This is her second illustrated book.

TABLE OF CONTENTS

INTRODUCTION

This is the second book in a series of five. The main character, Coco is now a sixth grader. After listening to the stories of her fellow classmates on the first day of school, she decides to lead a humanitarian project. With the help of her parents, the staff and students at Garrison Elementary, this project will become a welcomed blessing to those who need it the most. Best of all, the willingness of the students to help their fellow classmates exemplifies real altruism at a very young age.

1

The Ultimate
Presentation

The students began arriving at Garrison Elementary School at 7:30 a.m. on August 13, 2012. Coco Shantrel Dubois was one of those early arrivals. While moseying down the corridor, Coco hi-fived a few of her friends, who were mingling inside.

She stared at the plaque near the main office, which enclosed the inscription of the mission statement. It stated: Our purpose is to educate, empower, and inspire students to become successful in achieving their goals. After reading this declaration silently, she thought, "*I hope this last year will present new quests and opportunities for me to spread my wings.*

With this fresh mindset, Coco looked up toward the ceiling then surmised, *"The sky is the only limit beyond my reach."* Now she got comfortable and leaned against the wall near her classroom door. The young artist began reminiscing about last school years' assignment. It required creating a vision board, which she considered to be an inconvenience to her summer break.

That particular commission was given to her class on June 1, the last day of school. It bothered Coco so much that she couldn't rest until she got some things off her chest. When she came home from school that day, she shouted, "Mom and dad, let me tell you what that teacher wants the class to do over the summer!" By this time she was sitting on the edge of the sofa in the living room, all revved up and steaming like an engine.

Coco ranted on and on until she ran out of excuses. Her parents, Idris and Jasmine Dubois, listened closely to their daughter's complaints. Then they gave her this sound advice: "Daughter, learning how to do difficult things when it feels unnecessary is vital to your future. This project might seem like it comes at the wrong time, but if you finish the task, it will make you feel good about yourself and your accomplishments."

Coco enquired sharply, "Are you telling that I need to let this resentment turn into joy, so my personality will outshine the grudge that I feel?" "Yes, that's another way of looking at it," responded Jasmine. "Aright, I'll go ahead and do that ol' boring project," Coco mumbled.

Assuming that she couldn't disagree with her parents' advice, Coco arose from the sofa and went upstairs to obtain the list of supplies. This is that same list that she created on June 3, the morning after her slumber party. When the young designer

came downstairs, Jasmine took her on a shopping spree.

They arrived at Blossom's Fabrics about thirty
minutes later. This store had everything the young
designer needed to create her vision board. Coco
chose a variety of fabrics, batting, sewing notions,
a trifold cardboard, and ribbons. Then the two
of them headed home. Coco got busy sketching
styles of Pancake clothing, measuring, and trim-
ming swatches of fabrics.

Jasmine lent a helping hand by gluing the batting to the cardboard to give it a softer cushion.
Then Coco completed the rest of the vision board
by herself. These were her tasks: She chose the
ebony satin cloth to give the background a smooth,
glossy effect. Next she tucked the material under
the edges of the board and stapled it very neatly.

The final touches were attaching the swatches
of various textures such as Kinte cloth, seer sucker,
cotton, linen, velvet, rayon, and sateen to the board.

She also pinned the patterns of her Pancake designs to the black satin cloth, finishing with her handwritten labels to describe each item on the board. When everything was set in place, Coco took lavender ribbons and sectioned them in triangular patterns.

The pretty ribbons added more texture to the multi-layered areas. Her final touch was titling the vision board: *Coco's Unique Designs*. When she finished the board, she laid it on the top shelf in her closet that second week in June. Furthermore, that's where the project remained until today.

With those thoughts trailing behind her, Coco refocused her attention on today. She was joyful about her presentation this morning. It was her special gift to the world; a task that she had stuck with until the very end. This young artist's attitude had progressed from grappling with the project over the summer to transforming the most beautiful vision board ever.

As Coco stood against the wall, she felt the warmth of the sunlight streaming through the window. She soon imagined that the heavens had opened up to place a glow upon her countenance. That warmness inspired her to muse upon her parents' divine wisdom. They had given their daughter a chance to picture herself as a winner. Not only did they convey the purpose for creating this outstanding project, but also instilled an advantage for her victory over this mundane hurdle.

Even more, towards the end of her task, Coco realized that it was those (itty bitty) tidbits of wisdom that kept her on an even keel. She felt goose bumps on her arms whenever she pondered upon their inherent love.

The young artist inched closer and closer towards the locked classroom door. She desired to be the first person to walk into Ms. Ballard's room today. With her precious trifold vision board tucked safely under her left arm, Coco bowed her head and whispered, "It's now or never."

Enthusiasm was her energy; it had become a companion to her this morning. She was all charged up and ready to go. Any minute now, she just knew that Ms. Ballard would be coming to unlock her classroom door.

Out of the blue, Coco heard sounds of feet running swiftly down the hall. It was her bestie, Lyla, who bellowed loudly, "Hi Pepper!" Coco screamed back, "Hey Butter!" Both girls ran to each other and hugged tightly. Lyla whispered, "Let's see if Jill's name is on Ms. Ballard's list." Coco and Lyla's index fingers met on Jill's name. "Yay!" They shrilled when Jill's name was discovered.

Their smiles grew wider for they knew it was going to be a spectacular year for their trio. Jill was considered to be the comical one, who always brought excitement into the atmosphere. She was deemed as the "life of the party," which meant there was never a dull moment in her presence.

Coco and Lyla oozed with much exhilaration on this sunny morning. This threesome (Lyla, Jill, and Coco) had been in the same classes since the fourth grade. They were confidants, and their friendships were as solid as the Rock of Gibraltar. When they were in the fourth grade, these soul sisters made a pinky swear to stick together forever.

As these two besties stood chattering, they heard the sounds of clattering down the corridor. That fast click-clack noise was coming closer and closer to them. It was the noise of high heels hitting the tiled floor. To their surprise, it was Ms. Ballard scurrying around the corner like a flash of lightening. Mr. Taylor, the janitor, came along to with her to unlock her door with his master key.

Ms. Ballard had made several attempts earlier to unlock her door, but the tumblers within the lock didn't bulge. The lock finally clicked. The teacher and the custodian breathed a sigh of relief. "Thank you very much, Mr. Taylor," said Ms.

Ballard. Just before the teacher entered the classroom, she smiled at her students, Coco and Lyla.

When Ms. Ballard rushed into the room to turn on the lights, she proceeded to arrange her syllabus, roster, and teaching materials on the desk. This veteran educator had decorated her teaching environment with vivid colors and lots of educational charts for her students. These instructional charts will help to build cohesiveness in her classroom.

Like most English Language Arts teachers, Ms. Ballard prepared her lessons with oodles of accommodations. Her goal is to reach the students on every level in her classes. Each of the units were fun and challenging, which incorporated these six types of thinking skills: knowledge (awareness), comprehension (understanding), application (exercise), analysis (examining), synthesis (integrating), and evaluation (assessing).

In addition to brilliant teachers like Ms. Ballard, the Garrison Elementary staff has increased. There are now seven more new team members onboard, and the student body is more diverse than ever. For the first time, a dozen foreign students enrolled in this school. Their families have traveled from the four corners of the world. It is their first time arriving in the United States of America.

The main purpose of the newcomers traveling to the United States is to enhance their children's educational needs. Just then, three of those new foreign students entered Ms. Ballard's classroom. When Lyla and Coco saw them they were curious. Lyla said, "Ooh, I'd like to meet them and hear their stories." "Me too," replied Coco.

Before entering Ms. Ballard's classroom, a few familiar scholars greeted Coco and Lyla with a hand slap or a tap on the shoulder. Then the rest of the stragglers rushed into the room to take a seat before the tardy bell rang. Lyla and Coco trailed them; they took a seat in the third row, and left an empty chair for Jill.

Three minutes after the last bell rang, Jill came sliding through the doorway of Ms. Ballard's classroom. "I'm sorry for being late," uttered Jill. Ms. Ballard nodded and then smiled. Quickly, Jill scanned the room to find her besties. Her heart was filled with glee. "Whoopee!" Coco, Lyla, and Jill shouted as they hi-fived each other. Lyla motioned for Jill to sit next to her. "With pleasure," stated Jill as she reached over to give her besties a fist bump.

A bucketful of joy spilled over inside Jill's heart briefly when she saw Ms. Ballard's face. She admired this awesome educator very much. In the past school year, Ms. Ballard had the privilege of being their new teacher. She had deposited much love, wisdom, promise, and motivation inside her young scholars. Her favorite motto is: "Believe in yourself and remain confident!"

This awesome educator was also blessed to have been promoted to teach sixth grade English Language Arts (ELA) this new school year. This assignment required keeping most of her former students, which was just fine with Ms. Ballard. It was a pleasure for the young scholars to be under her amazing tutelage. She loved them as if they were her own relatives.

Ms. Ballard is a beautiful woman. She stands 5'5" tall without high heels. Her crinkled hair is always pulled back into a lovely bun. Currently, she sports brown and white zebra glasses with a gold inscription on the right temple. This educator speaks with a distinct Southern drawl, which is difficult to emulate. The students love to hear her speak; her vowels are exaggerated at times, but certainly delightful to the ear.

While standing in front of her desk, this confident educator began by stating, "Students, I am Ms. Joy Ballard from Tiffany, Georgia, and I have been teaching for twenty-five wonderful years. This is also my second year at Garrison Elementary School." Then the students clapped their hands to welcome their teacher, which delighted her, all the more. Then she asserted, "By the way, never call me by my first name."

Right away, Ms. Ballard picked up her floral pink and white roster from her desk and then initiated the roll call. When she pronounced Lyla's name, it sounded as L-e-l-a. This teacher had made an error in judgment by saying the "y" in Lyla's name as a long "e" sound. She knew her phonetic sounds well, but this time it came out wrong.

Evidently, that vowel sounded strange to Lyla's ears, and that made this preteen go bonkers. This incidence appeared to be a huge faux pas to 'Miss Picky' Lyla. For some mysterious reason, Lyla had gotten finicky about her name over the summer.

Lyla spoke up sarcastically. "It's L-y-l-a. The [y] is pronounced as a long [i]," she explained in a nasty tone. Ms. Ballard apologized to Lyla for that mistake, but Lyla just rolled her eyes and looked away. Jill and Coco gasped as they placed their right hand over their mouths. They couldn't believe what had just bellowed out of Lyla's mouth. Coco thought, "*I wonder what happened to my friend over the summer?*"

Furthermore, Lyla didn't give Ms. Ballard any mercy at all, **not even one apology**. At that point, the teacher turned her attention to finishing the roll call. She knew that something must have occurred for Lyla to become sassy; therefore, Ms. Ballard just shrugged it off this morning.

Out of respect for her classroom environment, Ms. Ballard flipped off Lyla's negative vibe as fast as she'd turn off a light switch. She walked in front of her desk to show Lyla who was "the boss" in her classroom. Without missing a beat, Ms. Ballard initiated a more pleasant dialogue with the rest of the class.

She inquired, "Class, please share with your classmates what you achieved over the summer break?" Two new boys, Jimmy and Cecil, raised their hands first. They over- talked each other continuously, trying to finish each other's sentences.

Cecil said, "Both of our fathers are friends, so they took us with them on Saturdays to do lawn work." Jimmy interrupted by saying, "But, I didn't like the heat!" "Me either," echoed Cecil. I kept pouring ice water on my head to cool off." That last response made everybody in the classroom laugh. Some students cackled like hens, while others slumped over on their desk with pain in their sides from chuckling so hard.

Betsy, a new girl, raised her hand intermittently between giggles. It was now her turn to enlighten her classmates. She stated, "Me and my mother sewed blankets for the homeless people. We handed them out at the Raven Center this summer." Ms. Ballard listened to all of their stories one by one.

Her countenance was glowing as she listened to her students' summer activities. She was glad that these enthusiastic students had been assigned to her roster. This ELA instructor's highest calling was to teach, motivate, and inspire these sixth graders to become more successful in their final year at Garrison Elementary.

When time drew near for Coco to share her new concept, she began tapping her finger tips lightly on her desk in a melodious pattern. She had developed a bolder personality, which was fresh out of the box. This year, there was no more doodling or ducking or dodging answering her teachers' questions. This new Coco Shantrel Dubois was focused, confident, and courageous, concerning her future vision. She had finally come into fruition, and there was nothing stopping her now.

In the next few seconds, this innovative artist will have the chance of a life time to express herself in front of her peers. It was a big role for Miss Coco to fill. Though, nobody had the power or magnitude to deliver this concept to the class in a sincere depth like this young designer. She was the sole creator of this quirky concept. None of Coco's besties could help her, even if they wanted, for this secret was hushed until today.

The young artist eased her right hand up half-way. She announced her intentions in this timid voice: "I would like to tell the class about my vision board." Ms. Ballard signaled for Coco to speak to her peers about her summer project. The young artist stood up in her row and began her speech. "I learned how to draw when I was only six years old, so every week I would practice. When I got better, I started sketching animals. This next story is kinda strange. I hope nobody laughs at me when I talk about it."

When Coco looked at her peers, she noticed that one of them was trying to sabotage her speech. It was William, a new transfer student, who started acting horrible towards her. He began sniggering, sticking out his tongue, and making silly faces at Coco. That situation caught her off guard. The young artist looked down at her feet as embarrassment swept her joy away in broad daylight.

That childish episode just about devastated her, but she snatched her joy back in the next two milliseconds. This blissful day still belonged to Coco Shantrel Dubois, and no self-seeking person was going to steal it from her at all. Not even some ol' transfer student who was just jealous. He had nothing better to do, but poke fun of others.

After that episode, the bold artist quickly focused her eyes on the teacher. She felt safer when she stared into the reassuring eyes of Ms. Ballard. It helped her to overcome the intimidation of those spiteful boys. Just as Ms. Ballard saw what was going on, she gave the rambunctious boys a stern look. They knew that look meant: *"Stop what you're doing!"* But somehow they didn't want to obey.

It was much better for them to make light of someone who was trying to express themselves, than to sit quiet and listen. Ms. Ballard motioned for Coco to bring her trifold vision board to the front of the class. "I want everyone to see your thoughtful labor of love," mentioned Ms. Ballard. The young artist propped her vision board upon the white board's ledge, and commenced to describe her ideas to her peers.

Thereupon, Coco extended her story with these words: "My new drawings came from the concept of my favorite meal, which is pancakes." Instantly, William hunched George, and George elbowed Felix, then Felix hollered, "Ouch!" Ms. Ballard stood by the three boys' row. She bent over and whispered, "Boys, I want you to show some respect to Coco!" Again, the teacher nodded at the young artist, which helped her regain more confidence.

Now Coco commenced to retell the story without any more interruptions from those playful boys. Her persistence was unwavering. She explained, "I've always loved eating pancakes for breakfast. One Saturday, my mom took me shopping for my birthday dress. When I saw the yellow dress with three tiers in the display window of Lyn's Boutique, I knew it was mine. I gave it this unique name – The Pancake dress. Right then, I asked my mom to buy that same dress for my birthday." She said, "Okay." "The next day, she ordered one for me."

Shortly afterwards, Coco showed her class-mates and Ms. Ballard a dozen Pancake draw-ings from her sketch book. Then she revealed the photos of her birthday party. These snapshots portrayed her girlfriends wearing lovely pastel dresses, and the fun that her guests were having on June 2, 2012.

Their activities including blowing bubbles from gum, eating all sorts of goodies, playing games, dancing, competing, and just enjoying each oth-er's personalities. Before wrapping up her story, Coco elaborated on the outfit that she wore today. She pointed to her clothing as she added, "My skirt has the same Pancake style as the yellow dress on the photos." The beautiful pea green, three tiered skirt was just darling on Coco. The matching pink and pea green, short-sleeved, ruffled blouse complimented the skirt very well.

Overall, the fifteen girls in Coco's class seemed very impressed with her presentation. Jurnee, one of the newer girls, thought to herself, *"Ooh, I like that outfit; I wonder where I can find a skirt like hers."*

When the presentation ended, Coco politely picked up her vision board and sat down gracefully. She placed the vision board on the floor between her and Lyla's desk. The class applauded for Coco's production as well as the other presentations. Then Jill and Lyla leaned over close to their friend, and they uttered quietly, ***"Yours was the ultimate presentation of all."*** Coco smiled and asked, "You think so?" "Yes, we do," responded Jill and Lyla.

Coco said, "I've been meaning to ask both of you this question, "Where are your vision boards?" Lyla put her left hand up to chin, and then replied, "I just couldn't bring myself to do it this summer." Jill stated, "Our family went on two trips this summer; I didn't have time to do that stuff!" "Uh-huh," Coco muttered as she snickered silently.

When the final applauses ended, Ms. Ballard walked to the white board to clarify her expectations for the school year. She grabbed the pointer to hover over the details of her syllabus. Then she said, "Class, this assignment is due tomorrow." Their first task was to look up a list of twenty verbs that were spelled out on the white board. This would help the scholars express themselves better in their writing projects. Then the teacher added, "I want you to create two sentences for each verb."

The students' voices reverberated, "Ugh, today?" Ms. Ballard stated, "You'll thank me later when it comes time to write several compositions." When the students heard the passing bell ring, they rambled out with their assignments tucked deep into their backpacks.

The verb assignment was overwhelming for Lyla, Jill, and Coco. Therefore, they wanted to do their vocabulary together at Jill's house. The three-some went to the office after school. They called their parents for permission to do their homework at Jill's house. Each of their parents felt that it was good idea for them to work together.

To comprehend their homework better, the trio decided to research the dictionary and the thesaurus for definitions and synonyms of their twenty verbs. The objective was for the students to place each verb in two different sentences. This assignment added up to forty sentences all together. The examples in the dictionaries aided Jill, Lyla, and Coco in writing better sentences, which was an added bonus for them.

Jill, Lyla, and Coco wrote different sentences, so they wouldn't be accused of copying off each other. They spread out in the den to give each other some space. The girls used three dictionaries and three thesauruses to give their work a personal touch. It took about an hour for them to finish their homework. The trio felt good about their accomplishments. Not only did they define the verbs, but they also gave an example with a synonym in the second sentences.

This was the first of many assignments that they would create together. After an hour of working diligently, they began to feel hungry. The trio finished their verb assignment and then waved goodbye. Lyla and Coco gathered their belongings and exited Jill's front door. The trio yelled out each other's nicknames: "See you tomorrow, Carma!" "See ya later, Pepper and Butter!" Jill (Carma) replied. Then Lyla (Butter) replied, "Bye, Pepper!" Coco (Pepper) replied, Bye, Butter!"

2

IMPLEMENTING THE PROJECT

When Coco opened her front door, she was on cloud nine. She could hardly wait to spill the beans about her first day of school. Jasmine, her mom, was just as anxious to hear the stories involving the students' summer vacations. "Let me hear the news," requested Jasmine. Coco entered the kitchen where her mom was cooking. She sat down on a brown leather barstool. Then she propped her feet upon the steel footrest.

Jasmine wanted to get a good earful of the story, so she finished boiling the potatoes, carrots, celery, peas, and zucchini. Then she drained the vegetables and placed them in a bowl to cool. Meanwhile, Coco yakked on and on and on. It sounded as if she hadn't taken a breath between her sentences. There was so much to tell.

Right then, Coco hurled a fantastic idea into the kitchen atmosphere as though she was batting for a homerun. This up-and coming- philanthropist hoped that her mom would permit her to run around the bases before striking her out on the home plate. Her unspoken subject made her a lil' nervous, which is why Coco's voice went into a high pitch.

With a squeaky voice, she said, "Hey Mom, there is a new girl in my class named Betsy. She and her mother made quilts this summer to cover homeless people in the winter time." Jasmine wondered where her daughter was going with this topic. "That sounds productive," indicated Jasmine as she squinted her right eye and wiped the sweat off her face.

Coco stopped talking abruptly to inquire, "Mom, can we do a special project for the less fortunate people at Garrison Elementary?" Jasmine replied, "That's sounds like a good idea. Let's discuss this subject with your father when he comes home from his dental office. We'll give him a few minutes to unwind from work before presenting this idea.""Alright, mom! I really want to do something special," Coco replied.

The young philanthropist got up slowly from the bar stool and then crossed her fingers behind her back. She was confident that her spiel had hit a homerun with her mom. After her father, Idris, came home and rested awhile, she pitched her new project to him. He said, "Coco, that's an excellent idea!" Coco shouted, "Yes!" Then she retorted, "I want to start with collecting pennies; I know some friends that will be eager to help me with it!"

Her dad said, "If you can collect 5,000 pennies, your mom and I will donate five hundred dollars to Garrison Elementary. Then he looked over his right shoulder to ask, "Coco, do you know how much five thousand pennies equals?" She thumped her forehead lightly with the three middle fingers on her left hand. Firing her answer off rapidly, she replied, "Uh, 5,000 pennies; I don't know, but I can figure it out!"

Then Coco went over to the writing desk in the living room. This smart mathematician sat down and began to work the numbers on a notepad. She knew her way around multiplication and division; it was her preferred subject in the fourth grade. She shouted out the answer quickly from the living room, "Dad, five thousand pennies equals fifty dollars!"

"Well done daughter," exclaimed her father wholeheartedly. Then he said, "Go into the kitchen to ask your mom to help you with the details. You need to have a plan on how you will be collecting the pennies." "Okay, dad," answered Coco. She had gotten the first approval, and it was an added blessing that her parents were willing to chip in with the Penny Campaign. Unbeknownst to her, she had inherited a gift of philanthropy from her parents.

Just now, Jasmine combined all the cooked vegetables with the beef roast to create the hash. Then she served their hearty dinner, which was comprised of hash, spinach salad, toasted bread, and iced tea.

Later on that evening, Jasmine articulated these instructions to her daughter, "I'm going to write a letter tonight. I want you to go to the office tomorrow and give Principal Quinn the letter from us. It is in reference to your Penny Campaign. Ask the principal if we can place a container in every classroom. Maybe Principal Quinn will allow you to use this project as a school-wide project, so that every student can get involved." "Okay, mom," answered Coco.

As promised, Jasmine wrote a letter to the principal. She typed the letter on ivory linen paper. The acronym "JCS" was just above her letterhead, which stood for Jasmine's Counseling Service. Then Mrs. Jasmine Dubois sealed the letter inside a self-adhesive envelope, addressed to Principal Quinn. When the envelope was handed to Coco, she hugged her mom with delight. Then she placed the note momentarily over her heart.

Afterwards, Coco sauntered into her father's study to give him a tight squeeze. This novel philanthropist knew that she could count on her parents for support. They had come through for her every time. What's more, this was a worthy cause; a win-win for everybody involved. She was ready now. This sensational zeal would last inside of Coco's heart until the morning. She imagined running around the bases several times with freedom, joy, and victory in her soul.

At sunset, Idris and Jasmine imparted another wonderful tidbit: "Coco, just in case you don't meet your goal, we'll still give five hundred dollars to Garrison Elementary School." That last comment boosted Coco's morale; she was eager to get this project on the calendar. She muttered, "I'm going to need all hands on deck from all my neighboring friends." "For sure, Sweet Pea," answered her parents.

On Tuesday, Coco went to the main office, and she requested to speak to the administrator, Principal Quinn. The principal came out of her office and shook her student's hand. Then she asked, "What is your name, young lady?" As Coco cleared her throat, the young philanthropist indicated politely, "I'm Coco Shantrel Dubois. I have something to give you." Then she passed her principal the note written from her mom.

While reading the heartfelt note, Principal Quinn became teary eyed. "Sure! It's okay to start a campaign to help the students, as long as it is a school-wide project. I'll talk to all the educators, and get every class involved. We'll place a container in each classroom. Come by my office at the end of the school day. I want to give your mom a letter stating my permission," declared Principal

Quinn. "Thank you very much, Principal Quinn," replied Coco.

This afternoon, Coco walked home alone. She whistled and sang, sporadically skipping over the cracks in the worn sidewalks. The second that this young philanthropist returned home, she dialed Lyla and Jill three-way on the phone.

Coco declared, "My parents are going to let me start a penny drive for the unfortunate kids to have a good Christmas this year!" Both Lyla and Jill got all excited. They inquired, "When can we start?" Coco answered, "I believe we can start on next Monday. Will you help me collect the coffee cans from our neighborhood this week? We will need about twenty-five of them for the teachers to collect the money."

Lyla and Jill shouted, "Yes!" Without hesitation, they got busy dialing and texting their friends from their surrounding community. The trio requested their friends to help them with this huge project.

They told their classmates to ask their parents if they could have any empty tin coffee cans that were ready to be tossed. If so, please bring them by our houses as soon as possible. Each classmate who lived nearby their neighborhood was delighted to support them in this project.

Jill, Lyla, and Coco were in a state of jubilation. Within two days, they had collected twenty-five tin coffee cans from their surrounding neighbors. **The friends within the community brought the largest empty tin coffee cans to the trio's houses via bicycles, mopeds, scooters, wagons, skateboards, go-carts, and on foot.**

Right away, Lyla and Jill and brought their collected cans over to Coco's house. Jasmine helped Coco paint the tin coffee cans various pastel colors throughout the week. When the cans were painted and dried, the mother-daughter duo labeled them: ***"Pennies for the Holidays."*** Then they wrapped pretty jewel tone ribbons around each can. Next

Coco slit a hole in the center of the plastic lids to permit money to drop easily inside the containers.

On the ensuing Monday morning, Jasmine drove Coco to school. They went to the office to seek the final approval from Principal Quinn. Coco introduced her mother to the principal; the ladies shook hands for a few seconds. Principal Quinn was in awe. She was so elated that one of her students had such an interest in another person's welfare.

Principal Quinn noticed the twenty-five cans that were separated between the two long-handled, red wagons. There was a sparkle in her eyes. She winked at Miss Coco Shantrel Dubois, and then exclaimed, "My, those cans are very beautiful! I believe the students at Garrison will be delighted to take part in this new project."

Principal Quinn kicked off the campaign and made the coin collecting competition official that day. She related to Jasmine and Coco, "I know this venture will be successful. You have my blessings." The mother-daughter duo smiled and thanked Mrs. Quinn.

Ms. Sally Niche, the principal's secretary, leaned over the counter to see the painted cans. She loved the colorful ribbons. Out of curiosity, she enquired, "Where did Coco come up with this idea of the coffee cans?" Jasmine replied, "You know my daughter; she is rather precocious for her age." The office staff grinned as they admired the new philanthropist's passion for her classmates.

After that compliment, Jasmine waved good-bye to the office staff. Then the mother-daughter duo pulled the two long-handled, red wagons with twenty-five decorated cans to every classroom. This project provided Jasmine a chance to meet the new staff at Garrison Elementary School for the first time. As Jasmine and Coco entered the teachers' classrooms, they welcomed them with an open heart and a handshake.

The mother-daughter duo entered the final classroom, which was Ms. Ballard's room. Coco was pleased to introduce her mother to her English Language Arts teacher. They greeted each other with a handshake and smile. Jasmine handed the teacher the last coffee can to place upon her desk.

Ms. Ballard said, "Thank you very much." Now Jasmine placed her hand over her heart and then kissed her daughter. She whispered, "Goodbye Sweet Pea; I love you." Coco smiled and then waved goodbye to her mom.

During this interlude, Ms. Ballard expressed the purpose of the decorated coffee can. Then she asked, "Class, will you be willing to bless families for the Christmas holidays by giving them one of the best holidays they will remember?"

The students replied in unison, "Yes!" "Okay, you may place loose pennies in this container any school day of the week. And by the middle of

December, we'll see how much we have collected," replied Ms. Ballard.

3

THE FIELD TRIP

During the month of October, Ms. Ballard desired to take her students on a field trip to visit the International Historical Museum. The purpose of this trip was to educate her students on indigenous civilizations. By mid-October, Ms. Ballard started preparing her Language Arts class for the trip at least two weeks in advance. The permission slips were sent out fourteen days prior to the trip. The student brought back their permission slips with the next three days.

October 15, 2012, the day of the field trip, came in with a nip. The forecast was partly cloudy and the temperature was 67 degrees. Since the weather was nippy, the students put on their jackets to stay warm. They lined up by the back entrance to wait for the teacher's signal to board the bus. One of the new students, Poppy, had been recently involved in a car accident. Hence, she had to use a wheelchair to get around from place to place.

Ms. Ballard guided Poppy to the wheel chair lift. Soon the platform raised her inside the bus. After Poppy was boarded and secured, the rest of the students ascended upon the yellow school bus. The bus driver was eager to take the children on their fun journey.

Once Ms. Ballard, the students, and the volunteers arrived at the International Historic Museum, the tour guides were divided into five groups with five students in each group and a volunteer. On one of the tours, the guide pointed to the reliefs that were displayed on certain walls. Poppy asked the guide, "What is a relief?" The tour guide paused the expedition and replied. "A relief is a sculptural technique where the sculptured elements remain attached to a solid background of the same material."

Surprisingly, the inquisitive Poppy, was satisfied with this gentleman's answer. She had never been taught that the word [relief] had another meaning. Poppy muttered, "Who would have thought that it had something to do with paintings, sculptures or drawings?"

While touring the museum, the students learned how ancient civilizations survived in earlier times with meager supplies and food rationings. Behind the glass windows, were rustic artifacts displayed inside boxes, and on top of shelves. There were numerous items on display in adjacent areas of the museum such as: old postage stamps, covered wagons, stage coaches, coin collections, masks, paintings, shoes, miniature dolls, clothing, blankets, and wooden furniture in different centuries, bow and arrows, ancient tools, and maps.

Amidst the relics were plenty of descriptions pertaining to their ethnic cultures. These ancient people were from these continents: Asia, Africa, Europe, North America, and South America.

As the tour guides led each section of students through the corridors, the students had a myriad of questions for them. A few of the students wanted to know what it was like to be without decent clothes, shoes, or food. There were also scholars who criticized the displays because they couldn't relate to those ancient times. During certain eras, people lived in igloos, huts, and shacks. They students didn't comprehend why men and women were nomads, or why they hunted and gathered food for their livelihood.

The three foreign students from Guatemala, Haiti, and India were deeply concerned about some of the displays. They had tears in their eyes and began to have discussions within their small group. The students talked about how important it was for families to stay together throughout hardships.

This was a touchy subject for them because of what they had seen with families in their own country.

For the most part, this museum trip touched the hearts of several children who had come from broken homes. At any given moment, their lives could be discombobulated. There were days when some students felt like they may be taken away from any normal life. Hence, remaining together through hardships was a phenomenon to the temporarily adopted, displaced, and/or latch-key students.

In reflection, a third of Garrison's students lived with only a mother or with a father or an orphan or foster mother. Whereas, there were also similar kids of ethnic groups, who lived with their grand-parents because either parent might have been deceased, unemployed, homeless, incarcerated or too ill to care for them.

Perhaps their lives might have been in sham-bles because of violence in their homes. Regardless of their situations, a few of these students, who were within these five groups, appeared to enjoy being on the field trip. These displaced students experienced a sense of belonging today — a part of something positive for a change.

The museum expedition had taken approximately three hours; it had now come to an end. The clock was ticking for the Garrison Elementary students to get back on the yellow school bus. Several elementary schools were touring the museum simultaneously from all over New Jersey. To keep the students safe, Ms. Ballard requested each volunteer parent to stay with the students in their group.

Soon after, Ms. Ballard had a student to push Poppy's wheel chair to the wheel chair lift. Once she was inside the bus, the teacher climbed the stairs and welcomed the rest of the students onboard. The parents ascended upon the bus after the last student. Ms. Ballard counted each student during the roll call. As she pronounced each student's name, they said, "Present!"

The teacher signaled for the bus driver to start the voyage back to the school. Before the school bus pulled off, the students began chattering about what they saw and how they felt. So far, it was a typical outing – the bus was fun, but noisy. As usual, the driver scolded the students for being too loud. Then he yelled, "No eating on this bus!"

The students picked up their candy and gum wrappers without any back-talk. They stuffed the trash into their pockets. William mentioned to George, "I don't think I could have survived back then." George replied, "Me neither!" Now a huge argument exploded like a cannon: Shannon, a new girl, snapped at William. She got all into his conversation and let him have a piece of her mind.

Shannon confronted her classmate with these words: "William, you think that you are better than other people! Those people barely made it back then. You get on your high horse and can't identify with anybody beneath you." William said, "Get out of my face, you ugly girl! I don't like you anyway, leave me alone! Every time I have something to say, you try to cap me off. Why do you always scold me for my opinion?"

At this moment, William's fists were balled up tightly, ready to strike her or anybody that said anything negative to him. Concurrently, Shannon was towering over William with her knee embedded in the seat, ready to sock him too. She was a bully, who enjoyed tussling with boys; she was always angry at them.

Shannon was so livid that her eyes enlarged with malice. The huge chip on her shoulder was as large as a boulder. This hostile, young girl enjoyed showing boys how threatening she was by challenging them. When the students on the bus saw this aggravated commotion, they chanted, "Fight… fight…fight!" That word sent off a danger to everyone. Ms. Ballard turned around quickly and heard the loud cacophony. It had burst into the air like a boom. She rushed to the back of the bus to intervene between William and Shannon.

Ms. Ballard spoke sharply, "I'm going to deal with both of you when we get back to the school!" She separated them into different rows by placing them on either side of two volunteer parents. This allowed them to cool down before they got to the school parking lot. Ms. Ballard felt that if they adjusted their temper, then it would keep them from being suspended or kicked off the bus for future field trips.

The bus pulled upon the back parking lot about 3:00 p.m. Upon arrival, Principal Quinn met her students at the back entrance and wanted to know how they enjoyed the outing. "We liked it," they said while nudging one another. Nobody complained about being tired of walking.

They didn't even discuss the tiff between William and Shannon. The students desired to go on more field trips. Ms. Ballard stood between Shannon and William. She whispered to the Principal that she needed to take care of a problem. Principal Quinn nodded and took the rest of the students inside the school to prepare them to go home.

4

THE COUNSELING SESSIONS

The next school day, Ms. Ballard sent Shannon and William to the school counselor, Mrs. Keita. She was from Mali. Not only was Mrs. Keita a counselor, but she was also a Child Psychologist. Her family had come to the United States when she was a young girl. Therefore, she grew up learning new customs and ideas in the United States.

Mrs. Keita was soft spoken and very gentle with the students. There was an aura about her that made the students feel safe. At noon, William and Shannon knocked on Mrs. Keita's door. The counselor studied their droopy faces. The look of remorse was upon their visage; they felt bad about what happened on the bus. Until now, they couldn't look the counselor in the eye for they were ashamed of their actions.

Mrs. Keita welcomed the students into her office by saying, "Come in and take a seat. I want the two of you to explain to me what occurred on the school bus yesterday." First, Shannon revealed her side of the story, and then William divulged his side of the incident. After acquiring that information, the counselor said, "I want both of you to watch a fifteen minute film on bullying.

When the film ends, we'll discuss some events that trigger negative emotions. William and Shannon replied, "Okay." As they sat down on the paisley upholstered chairs, the twosome looked around the counselor's office. This warm atmosphere caused these angry, troubled, youngsters to be at ease. They soon breathed a sigh of relief.

Mrs. Keita had a sequence of positive words portrayed on nine posters attached to the white walls. The titles that she had chosen for each poster were: Love, Joy, Peace, Long-suffering, Gentleness, Goodness, Faith, Meekness, and Temperance. On the opposite side of the room was a lavender accent wall. This light pinkish purple wall calmed the angriest individual who entered her room. Besides, this lavender partition exuded much love and peace to the instigator and innocent.

Mrs. Keita made several notations, while the students watched the short film. When the film ended, the Child Psychologist began her session with Shannon and William.

She said, "Shannon, tell me something sweet about your personality. Then tell me what ticks you off. William, I want you to answer the same questions after Shannon. Is that alright with the both of you?" Mrs. Keita asked calmly. Both of them answered, "Yes!" Then the counselor listened intently and took notes from each of them as they described themselves.

Mrs. Keita learned more information about William and Shannon's unhealthy lives. Shannon's parents were divorced parents. Her father had abandoned Shannon and her mother when she was only five years old. That incident devastated Shannon, and she never forgave him for leaving them.

For years, it caused Shannon to become hostile and irritated toward males. No one had ever counseled her relating to these unfortunate circumstances, which left her wounded. This chaotic young girl, had been lugging a bagful of anger, hostility, and bitterness for twelve years now.

Throughout the first session with Shannon, Mrs. Keita surmised that both Shannon and her mother needed family counseling. Thus, she decided to reach out to Shannon's mother about free counseling in her community. There was an agency that worked pro bono for people who were on a fixed income. The organization was located in their neighboring church.

As for William, he had an adverse situation. He was better off financially than Shannon, but his family's life was just as dysfunctional. Both of his parents were living together, yet his father was very controlling. He shouted at William rather than taking time to communicate with his son in a loving manner. His father gave him all the material things that he needed, but his he didn't deposit love into his son's soul.

William was hurting most of the time, except when he stole away to sing to himself. This was a decoy to declutter his mind from all the trauma that he experienced on a daily basis. Besides his mother's love, it was the second emotion that made him feel good. When he hummed, it took him into a healthy place where he felt loved and appreciated.

Periodically, William encouraged himself by reading the Bible. He had been given this price-less jewel on this past Easter. When he read the Bible, it was as though there was always a scripture that had his name written within the pages.

William interpreted this as God's ways of loving him through the hard times. Those were the nights that he didn't cry himself to sleep.

The missing ingredient in this young man's life was love. He yearned to have this natural affection from his father. Although, as far as his father was concerned, this emotional was conditional, but the money that he gave his son couldn't buy a pound of his love.

For that reason, William suffered badly from this lack of empathy. His mother felt helpless at times, but she continued to nurture her son with as much love as possible. William still felt a deep hole in his spirit; he yearned to fill it with an everlasting love.

Mrs. Keita sent home contractual papers for William and Shannon's parents to sign. She decided to counsel William and Shannon in her office at their lunch time. The counselor desired to help them learn behavioral techniques. This would not result in them missing any school activities. Both of them would spend an extra thirty minutes learning positive behavior towards themselves and others. Their total time with Mrs. Keita will be an hour three days a week.

William and Shannon were to bring back the contractual papers signed by their parents on the following week. Both students agreed to comply with the counselor and were glad that they didn't get suspended. Mrs. Keita documented her actions, and then she followed up with a phone call to their parents. It had to be before Friday's school day ended.

Both Shannon and William brought back their papers on the succeeding Monday. Their parents had agreed to allow them to have counseling for eight weeks during their lunch time. It also included spending an extra thirty minutes for discussions. This worked out wonderfully because both of them had the same schedule.

During the next eight weeks, Shannon and William will be learning how to develop positive behavior under the tutelage of Mrs. Keita. Their interventions includes using fidgets to relieve stress whenever they feel triggers swaying them to initiate bad behaviors. They have also been trained to think before responding negatively.

Besides that, William and Shannon are concurrently learning how to use intervention techniques via of these avenues: positive and respectful communication, showing humility in their body language, and learning to speak in a polite tone to their parents, relatives, staff members, and peers. Plus, they often practice role play with one another, so they can learn how to be more hospitable to each other.

The counseling sessions has helped William and Shannon in many profound ways. William has been turning his frustration into constructive reactions. Instead of lashing out, he is learning to count to ten silently before speaking. This will help him cool down and make positive statements. Using a punching bag in gym has helped him to get this resentment out when he needs a release. He isn't calling girls "ugly" anymore, nor does he want to beat them up when they provoke him.

As for Shannon's behavior, she is learning that getting back at males, who have a different opinion than hers, isn't the answer. Likewise, she knows that blaming males for her father leaving their family is unhealthy. Even though these actions will take years to fully develop, Shannon is willing to remain silent when she doesn't agree with someone. This helps her to regain her thoughts.

She writes down her feelings nightly in a journal, which permits her to release any hostility that has built up during the school day. This tool has become an asset to this meticulous, young lady. Nowadays, she has acquired a flair for writing. Shannon desires to become a famous writer in the future.

Her daily affirmation to herself is to not allow that green eyed monster, "envy," to control her anymore. Instead, Shannon believes that she can accomplish anything through prayer and forgiveness. This advice is what she has been taught through counseling at her local church. It has made a difference in her interactions with people. During the course of these eight weeks, Shannon and William are adjusting to their new behavior styles and being cordial to one another.

5

THE AMAZING MUSICAL

n Tuesdays and Thursdays, students travel weekly to the special classes such as physical education, art, and music. The music teacher, Ms. Haley teaches all of the students in the school. Most of the students enjoy coming to her class. This quarter, Ms. Haley is teaching kindergarten through sixth grade a new song that she wrote. It is titled: *"Being Grateful."*

This wonderful music teacher is reaching out to the multitude of quiet students inside the classrooms of Garrison Elementary. They are great singers. Their voices are so smooth that they sing acapella at times. Their vocal sounds are very pleasant in any range.

Alas, most of them just sit back and watch the audacious students go forth and sing aloud in the music class. They are often introverted and intimidated by their peers' talents. These talented singers compare themselves to anyone that they feel are better equipped than them.

Occasionally, their fellow classmates have heard them singing in the restrooms, on playgrounds, and around their neighborhoods. A lot of these talented students are standoffish. Their self-esteem holds them back. These shy children need someone in their home to help them trust their own instincts – to believe in them – and value them. As a result, these singers may begin to appreciate their precious vocal skills as gifts to society. Perhaps these singers will become great renowned vocalists in the world.

Ms. Haley discovers a few of these talented individuals in her music class each month. Their voices escape through the cracks in the room and flow with harmony. In lieu of this situation, she has prepared her class to be a nurturing environment. It is proven to be an asset to all students who want to learn better harmony or pitch.

It appears to everyone that the music class is "the setting" where students can literally be themselves. That's because Ms. Haley doesn't make students feel ashamed if their voices aren't up to par. She knows that every student isn't musically inclined, yet she helps them achieve a strong musical pitch. For that reason, some of these shy students are getting comfortable with letting their voices be heard.

Ms. Haley has been blessed with a special gift – the tenacity to work with timid students. She doesn't compare her students to each other, nor does she permit them to degrade each other in her presence. Each voice is precious, no matter how it sounds. "Humming can flow from anybody's soul. I always incorporate a singing or humming part for students in the smallest musical activity," Ms. Haley concludes.

At Garrison Elementary, the main theme is to give students a sense of belonging. Even though students may display behavior issues, Ms. Haley desires for them to remain in the music classes. She supports this adage, "Music is the gift that God gives us to appease our souls. The melodies in certain songs can bring peace to any chaotic situation."

This remarkable music instructor surmises that a playful student such as George will show more interest in music than language arts. In contrast, music encompasses the sounds of melodies and cadence, which speak to his natural way of understanding. He prefers mathematics; therefore, music is easier for him to grasp because he counts the beats.

George admits that he is better in playing the piano than he is in English. Often when he is called upon to read, he feels intimated because students have to hear him read aloud. If he stumbles over a certain vowel or consonant sound, he gets embarrassed. His piano skills, however, are at the top of a ten-chart scale, and he's taught himself to play skillfully by ear.

To help George learn more about music, Ms. Haley chose him to play the piano for the school's musical performances. She envisions George as a future maestro. By the end of the school year, she expects him to be reading and writing music.

One day William came to Ms. Haley's room to talk to her about getting into the choir. Until now, she hadn't mentioned anything to William pertaining to the musical, so she waited until he was ready to get involved. She had heard him project his voice last year. Thus, she knew how it flowed when he sang, and he would be an asset to the choir.

"You have a powerful tenor voice for a twelve year old. The audience needs to hear your gift, William. Singing is your best gift to present to the world," stated Ms. Haley as she spoke to William. "That's a nice comment, Ms. Haley. I've never heard anyone say those kind words to me," responded William.

"Well, take that compliment and tuck it in your heart; you need to believe it! William, you have what it takes to have a singing career in the future," asserted Ms. Haley. "Okay! I want to sing in the musical," demanded William. "Let's do it," responded Ms. Haley.

With the performances coming up soon, Ms. Haley decided to allow the boys to practice after school on Wednesdays. Every Thursday was set aside for the girls' groups. Coco, Jill, Lyla and a multitude of girls from different classes practiced their songs at three intermissions, fifteen minutes apart. Different groups of girls and boys sang these styles of music: pop, hip hop, classical, and gospel music.

Everyone was permitted to stay after school for an hour on those selected days. Some students practiced singing songs that had been assigned to them. Whereas, Coco, Jill, and Lyla had a special song that they wanted to sing for Ms. Haley. After numerous weeks of practice, the music teacher presented a school musicale for the entire school.

The musical was divided into three sections: Grades kindergarten through second grade went to the nine o'clock program. Grades third through sixth went to the second program. The Friday evening performance was held at seven o'clock.

This was scheduled for parents who worked in the daytime that couldn't take off work. This special time suited for them, who desired to support their children's endeavors. Jill, Lyla, and Coco also performed that night under the starry lights, in front of the black background. Their song was titled, *"Thanks for the Good Times."*

George played the piano for the entire musical. William sang solo to a song that he wrote while going through his struggles. It is titled, *"I know I Can Make It – With God All things are Possible.* His parents came on Friday evening to support him.

His father and mother were so proud of their son that they gave William an extra standing ovation.

Students from various classes sang, tap danced, and rapped a few songs, whereas some students played woodwind, percussion, and string instruments in the program. Shannon was one of the girls who played the flute. She was extremely gifted in this area. On that evening, Shannon made sure that her mother came to watch her perform.

Every student who was involved in the musical, got a standing ovation from parents, teachers, secretaries, and Principal Quinn. When the performances were over, the Duboises were on their way out of the auditorium. Then Coco heard someone cry out her name. It was William, the boy who ragged on her on the first day of school.

He said, "Hey, Coco wait up!" She pivoted around on one foot and replied loudly, "What's up!" As Coco stood there with her family, William articulated these words: "I'm sorry for the way I treated you in our homeroom class on the first day of school. I was jealous because you seemed to possess a confidence that I didn't have. By me being new at this school, I found it easier to pick on a smart girl like you. Please forgive me for acting rude when you were talking about your vision board. I really thought it was a good presentation, but I was just too stupid to see it back then."

Before Coco replied, she looked at her father and mother for assurance. They nodded for her to speak. She commenced to say, "William, I forgave you that same night when I went home. On August 13, 2013, I wrote this prayer in my diary: God, I don't know why the new boy, William, was mean to me today, but I forgive him. I hope he learns how to treat his classmates better tomorrow."

At that point, William reached out his hand for Coco to shake his hand. She extended her hand then added, "I accept your apology."

Idris commented, "Young man, it took a lot of guts for you to apologize. You did the right thing because when you need forgiveness, it will come back to you in good measure." William said, "Thank you sir." Soon everybody departed their separate ways.

6

THANKSGIVING BREAK

The day before leaving for the Thanksgiving break, several students felt that Ms. Ballard and Ms. Haley's classes were in a tied position with the Penny Campaign. Thence, in order to beef up the competition, these classes continued to drop more pennies into the coffee cans on the Tuesday before Thanksgiving Eve.

Every instructor counted their pennies daily after the students went home. They kept their tallies locked up as well as the containers. None of the students had an inkling of the final count. It had to remain a surprise for everybody. This Penny Campaign was a wonderful activity, which reeled in all the staff's anticipation.

One evening Principal Quinn had a private meeting with her staff after school. She communicated with her staff these concerns, "My ultimate goal is to bless students and their families. Therefore, I only want the recipients to know who is receiving the money at the end of this campaign." The staff agreed to her instructions. The principal didn't want any student to feel embarrassed because of their lack of food or shortage of money in their home.

As for the Penny Campaign, it required faith, trust, and love between every individual. The principal, educators, and students had a harmonious relationship. All of them pledged to do their best for the families in need. This accountability stemmed from brotherly and sisterly love, which was probably taught in some of their homes.

Trust and respect was demonstrated in a full circle. It transmitted from the principal to teachers, then from teachers to students and from students to students, and students to teachers, and from teachers to the principal. What's more, the educators implemented these life skills weekly: flexibility, respect, patience, kindness, sharing, endurance, compassion, trust, honesty, and self-control.

All of these life skills aided the students in developing the need to become partners with their fellow classmates. Likewise, they heard lessons like this from their parents or grandparents while collecting pennies: "Perhaps during this campaign, you may become your brother's keeper. You can learn how to connect with your classmates better, and you can be accountable for each other." A plethora of the students took heed to their relatives' advice and became best friends with one another.

At last, the students from all over the United States had gone home for the Thanksgiving holiday. It was a well-deserved vacation for everyone. Most students can hardly wait to enjoy their four-day weekend, so they can explore new things and travel to visit loved ones.

Concurrently, there are additional occurrences that perpetuate during this time of year. Thanksgiving most often comingles with cold days during this autumn season. The wind blows intermittent cool streams of chilly air into the atmosphere; thereupon, causing people to walk faster and wrap up in warmer clothing.

Ever more, autumn prepares itself for an annual presentation of colorful displays. The scenery is breathtaking throughout the United States. Autumn (aka fall) is a vibrant representative of time and change. The iridescent autumn leaves that beautify the trees are magnificent this time of year. Its foliage turns from green, red, orange, yellow, and then to brown.

Inevitably, the multicolored leaves fall upon on the grounds or on rooftops or anywhere they please. On a fine day, the autumn weather is pleasant; it also creates a rustic scene in certain areas of the U.S. The sunny days seem to be shorter; leaving less time to for kids to play outside or for parents to fulfill their assignments before sunset.

On the other hand, there is another certainty relating to autumn. It is well-known for producing chills, thrills, and frills. The chills are from the weather changing; thrills are induced by outdoor/ indoor playful activities, and most of all, frills are the result of extra embellishments sewn inside or attached to scarves, hats, gloves, coats, jackets, and boots for extra warmth and lavish styles, in which people love to coddle themselves.

At the onset of the Thanksgiving holiday, individuals enjoy spending time with their families, whether it is playtime, raking leaves, baking home-made cakes, pies or cookies. Plus, many individuals can finally catch on their favorite television shows with idle time on their hand. Best of all, it is always a period of reflection of how they have lived their lives, and the blessings that have occurred on their behalf.

Countless students from all over the world probably rest throughout their Thanksgiving interval, but not Coco, Lyla, and Jill. This trio didn't want to focus on idle time right now. Rather, their minds were on accumulating the most pennies in the school. They sought to win the big prize – a pizza party.

Like many students at Garrison Elementary, they had this same two-fold reason for wanting to be the winners. Principal Quinn told the students that the winning class would have a pizza party after the winter break. So, this trio prayed that their class would become the winner. In their spare time, they were going to discover as many coins as possible.

Wherefore, Jill Lyla, and Coco learned more ways to collect money over the fall break. They found pennies on the streets, floors, sofas, chairs, and in unfamiliar places. One of those places was the supermarkets. Whenever they went shopping with their parents, these girls searched for loose pennies on the floors of the stores. Jill found a string of pennies nearby a gutter on the street. She dusted them off and put them in a bag to wash them later.

The threesome discovered pennies that dated back ten years ago. Another funny thing transpired, the trio resorted to emptying their own penny banks. It was a pleasure to rattle that old porky pig for some loose change. While chatting three-way on their phones one day, the trio laughed about depleting their piggy banks. That's how much they wanted to win the pizza party.

Now that Thanksgiving was a day away, the Duboises made a concerted effort to reflect upon the purpose of this celebration in the US. This year, Coco's family made a special effort to discuss the word, thanksgiving. Jasmine expressed to Coco that thanksgiving is about gratitude. "We are to be grateful for the smallest blessings," she added.

Subsequently, Idris read aloud the purpose of why the United States celebrates this holiday. This conversation helped their daughter to relate to who, what, when, and why this celebration came into fruition. Coco learned more about the Pilgrims, who landed in Plymouth, Massachusetts in 1620.

She paid more attention this time. The sixth grader learned valuable information about the indentured servants, who arrived with the Pilgrims on the Mayflower. The first Thanksgiving was celebrated in 1621 at the Plymouth Plantation.

In addition to this, there was another tradition that Jill, Lyla, and Coco's parents indulged in occasionally. They took turns hosting dinners on special occasions such as Thanksgiving and Christmas. This year, the Thanksgiving celebration will be hosted by Lyla's parents. Since the three families resided in a cul-de-sac, it was easier to pack food from house to house. This Thanksgiving was promised to behold the best meals ever.

Lyla's parents, Zoe and Abeo Yusef, resided right in the center of the cul-de-sac. They were eager to introduce new Nigerian and English cuisine to their neighbors. Whereas, Jill's parents, Carmela and Jonas Samaras, were just as delighted to put on the show as well. In conjunction, Jasmine and Idris Dubois was going to create dishes as a five star restaurant would prepare. Each of the three families agreed to bring samples of their most delectable meals of their heritage to the banquet.

On Thanksgiving Eve, the three neighboring families were the chefs and sous chefs in their own kitchen. Their ranges were set on the right temperatures for baking, frying, steaming, and roasting. All of the men in each family adored foods from their native land. There was going to be an abundance of delicacies to indulge in again and again on Thanksgiving Day. The extravaganza was set for 2:00 p.m. on Thursday, November 22, 2013.

The Fabulous Thanksgiving Extravaganza

The fabulous Thanksgiving extravaganza commenced around 2:00 p.m. The hosts, Abeo and
Zoe Yusef (Lyla's parents), placed an array of delicious Nigerian foods upon their eight foot, claw-
footed oak table. It was decorated in an orange,
green, and yellow motif, which displayed matching
cloth napkins and a gorgeous centerpiece.

Zoe placed her finest china, stemware, and
finest stainless steel flatware on the orange tablecloth. The Yusef's contribution to the meal were
these foods items – Roasted Turkey, Jollof Rice,
Fried Plantains, Moi-Moi, Pepper Soup, Starchy
Vegetables, Puff, and Pound Cake and Vanilla Ice
Cream for dessert.

Jonas and Carmela Samaras (Jill's parents)
knocked on the front door at 2:05 p.m. Their contribution to this feast was: Paidakia, Moussaka
(meat, potatoes, and eggplant casserole), and
Baklava for dessert. "Where do you want us to

set these foods," asked Carmela. "You may place them right here in the middle section of the table," replied Zoe.

Then Carmela commented on the arrangements and décor in the dining room. "This table is just splendid," Carmela said. "Thank you," responded Zoe. Now the final guests arrived at approximately 2:07 p.m. Idris and Jasmine were at the threshold of the Yusef's living room door.

Idris tapped on the front door with the metal door knocker. Abeo greeted Idris and Jasmine at the door with these words, "Come on in my friends," he expressed. Idris and Jasmine pushed their green, two tiered rolling cart with heated bags of food to Lyla's parents' house. The Creole and Trinidadian aromas of ethnic food lingered around the cool climate.

Abeo took the heated bags from the Duboises and set them on the table. Zoe removed the luscious foods from the bags. Then she blended these final items amongst the other delicious foods. The Duboises created these dishes: Curry Duck, Fried Saheena (spinach and split pea batter), Macaroni Pie, and Coconut Bake for dessert.

The three couple's children, Lyla, Jill, and Coco came downstairs from Lyla's room. Jill and Coco came over to Lyla's house earlier in the day to talk on their cell phones to their classmates. Now it was time to hang up the phones, so they could take part in the bountiful feast.

Zoe rang a soft dinner bell for the guests to be seated around the table. When all nine banquet individuals sat down on the oak, claw-foot chairs, there was one empty seat. Zoe and Abeo always kept an empty seat at their table for anyone to needed a meal, especially around the holidays.

This was the Yusef's way of giving back to the homeless or any deprived person that may knock on their door for a meal. There was so much food on the table that the girls were overwhelmed. So, the trio (Butter, Carma, and Pepper) took a little spoon of this and a little spoon of that to satisfy their picky appetites.

On the other hand, their parents filled their plates with joy and delicious cultural foods. No one counted calories today for these circle of families ate until they were content. It wasn't just the meal that these three families enjoyed, but it was also the fulfilment of their diverse cultures and languages. They just liked hanging out together and loving on one another.

Now each person sitting at the table, bowed their head to give thanks to God for his goodness. That's the essence of what these neighboring families are grateful for this Thanksgiving Day – God's love for mankind.

7

THE PENNY CHALLENGE

When the month of December arrived, the rigid cold blasts of air were saturated with great expectancy. The children and adults at Garrison Elementary were filled with more suspense. This merry season had come forth with a gift, and a lift of excitement simultaneously.

Each homeroom teacher had this commonality that united them. The Penny Campaign snowballed into a victory lap for their students, regardless of their station in life. It had built more community amongst the Garrison population than any other group effort. Individuals were getting along much better because of this positive incentive. There were no more physical fights or heated arguments recorded.

These sagacious educators at Garrison Elementary had cheerfulness in their hearts too. They were in the final phase of this activity. Opportunity had arisen for them to count all the pennies before leaving for winter break. Even though these teachers had tests to be given, that had to wait until this event was over. On a scale of one to ten, this event was just as important as placing a score on a paper.

In just a few days, the quarter will be coming to a close. There are a number of students who are antsy about their letter grades. It is mostly the students who have lollygagged half of the school year. The gifted and talented kids thought they had a "shoe in" when it came to music and art. Besides that, there are several pupils who have been goofing off in Science and Social Studies too. They could be grounded over the holidays, even into the new school year.

Garrison's Penny Challenge had ballooned into a magnificent event. Excitement tapped lightly on every classroom door this morning to give a warm greeting. The expectations of winning were at the summit of every student's thoughts. At times, it was difficult for students to sit still in their seats.

They were as antsy as a toddler waiting on a bowl of his or her favorite ice cream. Their thoughts were, *"Did we win? Or who's going to get to have the pizza party?"* Everyone knew that in a few moments, time would reveal the correct answer.

On this joyous morning, the homeroom teachers took the decorated coined cans out of their locked closets. As soon as the daily announcements were read, the teachers did their final count. Principal Quinn requested the count of each homeroom on the loud speaker.

She inquired about the exact amount in random order. Each homeroom teacher shouted out how much his or her students had collected.

Ms. Ballard's class was the last one on the list to give an account of all their pennies.

When the principal called for Ms. Ballard's class, all her students yelled, **"Five thousand pennies!"** Ms. Ballard's entrepreneurs had accumulated five thousand pennies in five months. As Coco and her friends gave each other high fives, they shouted, "Yay!"

Suddenly, every single student leapt out of his or her chair, circling the room like a pack of bull terriers. Even the quiet learners, who never made hilarious noises, were screaming to the top of their lungs, "Hip-hip Hurrah! We did it!"

Principal Quinn came back on the loud speaker and recognized everybody for helping families at this time of year. She explained, "There are so many families that will be helped this season. Thank you for your acts of kindness. It will mean a great deal to these families. Students and teachers, you have shown everybody that you care. I'm going to do something special for every student when we come back from our Christmas vacation!" After Principal Quinn stopped talking, the entire five hundred student body yelled, "Yes!"

That same day, Coco's parents, Jasmine and Idris Dubois, kept their promise. They donated to the collection in the amount of five hundred dollars. Moreover, the Duboises decided to give another five hundred dollars to a Mission Organization. Idris knew just the organization that they should give this fortune; it would be appreciated gladly.

Principal Quinn announced Coco's name on the intercom. She requested for her to come to the office after the last bell rang. The principal told Coco that she had spoken to her parents about the collected amount. "When you get home, your parents will tell you about our decisions, mentioned Principal Quinn. "Yes, ma'am," replied Coco.

At that point, the principal explained to the young philanthropist, "The families that we decided to donate the monies to will be kept secret for their benefit.""Yes ma'am; I understand," answered Coco. She knew in her heart that those students' names had to be kept secret, so it wouldn't embarrass them.

Coco's main objective was to help people who may be in a crisis this time of year. When the young philanthropist came home, Jasmine told her what the principal relayed to them. We decided, along with Principal Quinn, to add all the currency together.

The money will be shared among ten families within Garrison Elementary School. Each family will receive seventy-five dollars for their household needs. Coco was elated that the gift of giving had involved so many caring people in her school.

The weekend prior to Christmas break, Jasmine heard from The Benevolent Mission Organization. That was the place where Idris' dental office had donated five hundred dollars. The Benevolent Mission noted, "We have never seen such love from a dental office. Thank you for all your effort. We'll be able to give out more funds to the people this year."

"It was our pleasure," responded Jasmine to the clerk at The Benevolent Mission Organization. Coco overheard the conversation and felt ecstatic about her parents' decision to spread the love around to this organization. Jasmine shared this information with Idris when he came home. He was euphoric to hear that compliment.

Coco was very proud because she was an heir to a family of such philanthropy. Her parents helped families all over the world who were in need. These types of charities are what the Duboises considered to be an asset to life – caring for the orphans, widows, and homeless, and anyone in a crisis.

8

THE CHRISTMAS SURPRISE

In America, the students were out for two weeks for the Christmas holiday. Some of Coco's friends went out of town for Christmas. But Lyla and Jill stayed in town. Coco's best friends telephoned her the first Saturday of the winter break, "Pepper, do you want to bundle up and go skating down the sidewalk?"

Coco stated, "Girls, wait just a minute." Then she hollered, "Mom and dad, may I go skating on the sidewalks with my friends?" They answered, "Yes, but wear your heaviest coat!" "Alright," answered Coco. She put on her hooded navy parka and white-laced skates. Then she rolled down the sidewalk and met up with her buddies.

The temperature in New Jersey was thirty degrees. This northeastern state seemed colder in the wintertime. The trio knew that they had better enjoy their skating adventure before the sleet and snow appeared. Slowly, Jill, Lyla, and Coco rolled down the sidewalk in their white-laced roller skates. Soon they knocked on more of their friends' doors around the corner.

Ai, Sasha, Malia, and Michelle lived on Tillis Court; this is the street behind Cinnamon Street. Lyla asked these four friends, "Can y'all come out and skate with us for a little while?" Each of their friends asked their parents for permission. All of their parents echoed the same answer. "It's okay. Make sure to bundle up tightly and come in before the sun goes down."

The four girls put on their neon skates and parkas, and then rolled down the sidewalk to meet up with Lyla, Coco, and Jill.

When the skating event was over, the seven pack of girls – Coco, Jill, Lyla, Sasha, Malia, Michelle, and Ai, assembled in a huddle. They all were bundled up in scarves, hats, and parkas. The cold air zipped in and out of their mouths and noses as they inhaled and exhaled.

The seven girls shivered and hugged each other for comfort. Eventually, the besties began to discuss their upcoming school events. It was evident that these comrades could possibly be separated into different middle schools next year. None of them desired to see that happen.

Michelle inquired, "Does anyone know what middle school you will be attending next school year?" The rest of the girls said, "Not yet!" Now the seven lassies' eyes got watery. The fear of being split up into different middle schools was too overpowering to their young minds. They wiped the tears away with their hands and cleared their throats.

All at once, the chilly air swooped down and whistled, "Whoosh," as it infiltrated the girls' clothing. It stung their noses, fingers and toes. That uninvited, icy airstream abruptly ended their in-depth conversations, and now it got the best of them. Then the group of seven misses embraced each other until the next gathering. Now shivering uncontrollably, they uttered, "Ciao," as they hurried home to warm up by their cozy fireplaces.

A myriad of new lessons were soon to be learned in the Dubois household. Whilst Coco was on her winter break, Jasmine taught her the basics of hemming a garment. Adapting to sewing with a needle and thread was the first rule to sewing. It was a must-have rule. This learning curve took the "up-and coming designer" a few times to get the hang of it, but she overcame with a little more patience than she desired.

Coco threaded the eye of the needle with a single strand. Even though she poked herself several times with the needle, she soon got the gist of it.

The novice seamstress really desired to master this simple, but tedious technique. Now she pulled the black thread through the eye of the needle. "Whew," Coco sighed when she succeeded. Lastly, Coco tied a single knot at one end of the single strand.

"Mom, I got it!" The novice designer expressed with joy. This was a great opportunity for Coco to learn how to slip stitch a dress. Jasmine showed the young seamstress on how to turn the garment inside out. Then she advised her daughter to place the thread under the black dress's hem and lift it up. "Stretch out the single strand with your right hand, Jasmine said.

The young seamstress said, "Mom, I did it again!" Jasmine told her daughter to keep the thimble on her right index finger so the needle wouldn't prick that finger again. "That's neat… let's do more later on," Coco exclaimed after she finished. Now she draped the dress across her arm and brought it upstairs. Next she placed it on a black velvet hanger in her closet. The young seamstress stood back and admired her work. Being an only child had its special moments. Normally, Coco gravitated towards activities with her friends, but this was a different season for the young novice. She was developing into a secure young lady.

Ah! Spending more time with her mom was a treat. So, on Sunday afternoon, Jasmine and Coco went to the mall to eat burgers, French fries, and malts. After the clerk handed them their strawberry malt, Coco seized two pink and white striped straws. Then she placed them inside the tall vintage glass filled with strawberry malt.

The mother-daughter duo slurped the first flavor of their malt together from the same vintage glass. Then Coco wanted to see which one of them could drink the fastest from that same tumbler. Jasmine agreed to the challenge. Coco said, "Ready, set, go!" Coco slurped up the malt in a quick, and she won the contest.

Jasmine commented, "You swigged that malt down faster than the water plunges within Niagara Falls." Coco laughed out loud at her mom's good hearted loss. This was Coco's special day. The mother-daughter duo was having a ball pigging out on whatever they imagined this afternoon. This keepsake moment inspired Coco to etch it in her memory forever.

When she arrived home, she wrote about their special outing in her diary. Then she went down to the kitchen. Coco was always finding new things to taste, so this month, she had acquired a new craze. It was pomegranates. The seeds tasted so juicy and delicious. Whenever she bit into the kernels, the juice spilled out and filled her mouth with purplish liquid. That was the fulfillment which she enjoyed faithfully.

In all her maneuverings, Coco had figured out another way to distract the juice from the red, hard shell of the fruit. She placed the pomegranate on a wooden cutting board and cracked the hard shell open with a meat tenderizer. Promptly, she dug out the seeds within the clusters and ate them in bunches.

"Mmm, this taste delicious!" Coco thought, as she crunched on those juicy seeds. Eating the seeds and spitting them out reminded her of sunflower seeds. Whenever she ate the pomegranates, they'd accidentally land on the floor. But she had to mop up the seeds before her mom saw this disaster on the tile kitchen floor.

Just now, while Coco was chewing the pomegranate seeds, she focused on Christmas. It was approaching much too fast. She desired to create something really special for her parents and grandfather's Christmas gifts. It had to be original and comforting. This afternoon when Coco and her mom were at the mall, she saw three ornate boxes that peeked her interest. Whenever the time came to buy gifts, she wanted to buy the boxes with her allowance money.

When the selfless artist studied the three ornate boxes, she reflected upon her loved ones' personalities. The black one with zebra stripes was for her father. The salmon box was for her mother, and the ivory box was for her grandfather. Coco had to figure out the type of paper to line the interior of the boxes. She did some brainstorming.

It had to be a substance that could withstand years of aging. It wasn't too long before she remembered what her art teacher revealed about acid free paper. This type of paper didn't yellow over the years. She knew that within ten years or more, the paper would still look brand new.

Later on that evening, Coco went into the living room to hang out with her mom. Then she asked, "Mom, may I go Christmas shopping with you. I want to go to that specialty store in the mall.""Okay," answered Jasmine. The subsequent day, Jasmine permitted Coco to go with her earlier in the day. Jasmine didn't want her daughter would see what she was getting her family for Christmas.

As promised, Jasmine took her daughter to Ziggy's Specialty Shop. Coco had the clerk to place all the art supplies in an opaque bag after she purchased them. Then Jasmine took her home so she could finish Christmas shopping for her family. Coco ran upstairs to line her boxes with the acid free paper. Next she filled the boxes with a collage of school events that transpired this year.

Around noon, Coco voiced to her father that she wanted to prepare lunch. Idris said, "Let me know when it's ready!" Coco believed that a tuna sandwich was an easy meal. She thought, "What can I pair with the tuna that will taste good together?" The novel chef thought, *"I'll just make the best lemonade that my dad ever tasted."* Now she opened the refrigerator to take out seven lemons. Then she removed a large glass pitcher from the cabinet, and gathered the sugar, plus the measuring cup.

Lemonade was a snap for this novice chef. It only took about five minutes to make. A week ago, Jasmine had demonstrated how to roll the lemons on the wood cutting board until they were soft. Then she sliced the lemons crosswise. That way, the circled slices could fit easily inside a glass with the wide sections visible.

Jasmine taught her daughter some safety tips such as how to hold the lemon with her finger-tips. Then she showed her how to use the opposite hand to stabilize the lemon on the board. This idea would prevent the lemons from slipping off the cutting board; therefore, she wouldn't cut her fingers. Coco's father liked his lemonade tart; not too sweet. So, she scooped about a cup of granulated sugar into the large pitcher of water with lemons.

She stirred it slowly with a rubber spatula. Secondly, the novice chef prepared the lemonade with lots of ice – just the way her dad liked it. There was one last treat that her mother imparted to her pertaining to decorating the lemonade glass: She'd say to Coco, "Save a few of the circular lemons to garnish the rim of the glass."

At that point, Jasmine showed Coco how to cut a slit in the center of the lemon's skin and flesh. The she placed it on the top of the rim of the glass. It gave the glass of lemonade a fancy look like the way the chefs do at the restaurants.

Coco obeyed her mom's instructions about the lemon garnish. She articulated to her dad that the lunch was ready. "Dad, I've prepared the lemonade just the way you like it – tart; not sweet. She had set each of their sandwiches on two pretty pink and white saucers, and their tall glasses of ice cold lemonade on the counter.

Now it was time to indulge. When Idris and Coco entered the kitchen area, they sat on the brown leather bar stools. "I like this lemonade," stated her father. Idris complimented his daughter further by saying, "This meal is very good!" The young chef replied, "I'm glad you like it, dad."

Jasmine rushed through the front door swiftly. She shouted, "Family, I'm home!" Idris and Coco were watching a family movie in the den. Jasmine knew that she had to dash into different rooms to hide her Christmas gifts. She soon spread the presents in areas that nobody would dare to search.

In a little while, Jasmine strolled into the den to relax in the soft amethyst lounging chair. She began to probe her family's minds, "What do you want to eat for dinner?" Coco and her dad chimed in unison, "Tonight we are going to help you cook dinner. Then we'll help you start Christmas dinner."

Jasmine was swept off her feet with those kind words. The family decided on sloppy joes and coleslaw with lemonade. After finishing dinner at the kitchen bar, Coco assisted her dad in washing dishes. They placed them in the dishwasher and listened for Jasmine's instructions. She communicated with her sous chefs which ingredients to remove from the pantry for creating the pies and cakes.

Baking from scratch was Jasmine's expertise. When she was twelve years old, her mom taught her how to cook just about everything. For this reason, the Duboises ate most of their meals at home, except for those special occasions.

At this interval, Jasmine decided to make Idris's favorite dessert – applesauce cake. When that cake tested done, Jasmine baked a German chocolate cake and then a lemon meringue pie. Her version of the lemon meringue pie was her daughter's favorite. When the lemon meringue pie was done, the sous chef took pleasure in the height of her mom's pie.

Miss Coco Shantrel was also partial to the tartness of the lemons, and the smoothness of the custard filling. But then, nothing topped the golden brown meringue; it was the prize in Coco's eyes. That egg-white/sugar/whipped confection with mounds of stiff curls atop the lemon pie, was the first taste of goodness in her mouth. The delicious meringue melted in her mouth, as she devoured it slowly.

Alas, nightfall had consumed their cooking time. Jasmine and her family had to get some rest for the evening. Before retiring, Jasmine prepared the turkey and set it in the refrigerator. Then she went to sleep until five o'clock that next morning. At the break of dawn, Jasmine allowed the turkey to get to room temperature before placing it inside the preheated oven. Meanwhile, she started to assimilate more recipes into the Christmas meal. Only a few more things had to be cooked, such as Efo Riro, Cassava, and Jollof rice.

Coco and her father arose from sleeping. The descended downstairs to help with the meals. Jasmine desired to teach her daughter a new cooking technique – making cranberry sauce. Idris gave Coco a bag of whole cranberries to pour into a pot of boiling water. The sous chef placed the cranberries in the pot and boiled them in a small amount of raw sugar with orange juice and a hint of allspice. She let them simmer for about ten to fifteen minutes.

After the berries cooled, Idris handed his daughter a shiny copper mold to pour the cranberry sauce inside. She sprayed the inside of the mold with cooking spray, and then she poured the cranberry sauce into the mold. Now she placed the cranberry mold into the refrigerator to chill for a few hours. This was Coco's first time actually cooking with her mom and dad during the holidays.

She felt grown-up on this Christmas Eve. This school year, she had developed a new attitude about cooking. At this phase in her life, she was eager to learn new things in the kitchen to become more productive. It was also her chance to give back to her parents for helping her with the Penny Campaign.

She asked, "Mom, what's next?" Jasmine directed her daughter to take a break. She said, "I want you to set the Mahogany dining room table with a white lace tablecloth for Christmas. Then I want you to arrange all the china, goblets, and silverware on the laced tablecloth."

Coco went into the dining room; she gathered all the items from the Mahogany china cabinet. She touched the gold and white fine china ever so delicately. Now the young designer set the plates, saucers, bowls, butter dish, platter, sugar and cream pitcher, gravy bowl, forks, spoons, knives, and gold trimmed goblets on the table in groups of three.

After the table was adorned with the beautiful dishes and silverware, the Duboises went upstairs to get dressed for their spectacular Christmas meal. Thirty minutes later, they came back downstairs to partake of their delicious meal. Idris pulled out the dining room chairs for his wife and daughter to sit down. Then he preceded to bring the entrée and the desserts from the kitchen into the dining room on a three tiered gold rolling cart with glass shelves. Soon after, Idris placed the Christmas meal on the lace tablecloth. The table setting was set perfectly.

Coco had been taught by her mother how to set a table for a king and queen.

After they blessed their food, the Dubois family reflected upon their accomplishments throughout the year. Coco was the sole heir to the wisdom that her parents possessed. She knew how to give, love, share, and have empathy for the downtrodden. When the Duboises dined this Christmas, they felt good for they had blessed someone else first.

Idris thought momentarily about the Golden Rule located in Matthews 7:12: It states, "Do unto others, as you would have them do unto you." This scripture meant a great deal to him and Jasmine. It gave him and his wife comfort when they gave to individuals or organizations. Idris would always tell his family, "You never know when you may need a helping hand."

Just after the Dubois family finished with their scrumptious meal, they rested in their comfy living room. This year the Duboises averted from their usual way of presenting gifts. Instead of opening their presents early in the morning, they decided to wait until later in the afternoon. Now Jasmine enquired if they were ready to open their gifts.

"Yes, we are," responded Coco and her father. Jasmine went into her room immediately to get the gifts. She handed Coco her gift first. As her daughter tore the paper off the long rectangular box, there was a gasp in the room. Coco was soooo overjoyed; she had received an abundance of sewing notions for the first time this year. It was just what she needed to launch her designing career.

This Christmas, Jasmine had given Coco a huge box of sewing necessities. There were packages of needles, miscellaneous colors of threads, patterns in her daughter's size, thimbles, a tape measure, and a sewing box, among other sewing notions. Coco reached over and gave her mother a big fat kiss, right smack on her left dimple.

Idris went into a room upstairs and brought down his packages. He gave Jasmine her gift first. It was a watch that glowed in the dark. Then he handed Coco one of her gifts. It was a silver charm bracelet with charms dangling.

Idris draped the bracelet around his daughter's wrist then fastened it. The charms had her best friends' names on them, along with her name. Idris expressed to Coco that more charms could be added later. "Alright, I like that," voiced his Sweet Pea as she shook her wrist to see the charms dangle.

Now it was Idris's turn to receive his presents. Coco presented her gift first. She handed him a medium size box. He unwrapped it and then exclaimed, "Ah, I really like this!" The zebra striped box was composed of fun-filled photos with the things Coco had crafted in the art room. Idris gave his daughter a big hug, which left a huge grin on her pretty face.

Coco handed her mother a very special present. She had filled a salmon box of mementos with crafty items, but somewhat different from her father's gift. Jasmine loved her gift. "Thanks, Sweet Pea," exclaimed her mom. Coco smiled and nodded her head in agreement.

In the blink of an eye, the great Christmas surprise was now ready to be presented. Idris had one more loving gift to bestow upon his wife and daughter on this special day. He handed Jasmine and Coco their gifts slowly at the same time. His instructions were: "Please open this box gently." Both Coco and Jasmine opened their gifts very softly, trying not to rip apart the white paper on their box with the huge red bow. The suspense was too much for Jasmine and Coco.

Suddenly, the mother-daughter duo was surprised beyond measure. "Jasmine said, "What!" Then Coco mimicked her mother's remark, "What!" Idris's favorite girls had received tickets to fly to Trinidad. "When can we travel?" Jasmine asked with tears in her eyes. Idris said, "We have open tickets to travel whenever we get ready to go." Then he asked, "When do you want to go?"

Coco responded instantly, "What about next summer when school is out? I'll be going to the seventh grade, and I will have a lot to tell my friends about Trinidad."

Idris asked, "Is that okay with you, Jasmine?" "That is perfect," replied Jasmine. The Duboises had another six months to think, plan, and prepare for their vacation next summer. Idris and Jasmine mailed their rare coin collection to Idris's father in Trinidad, a week before Christmas.

Whereas, Coco decided to give her grandfather his ivory gift box in person. She looked forward to being in the presence of Grandfather Jeren in his native land. *"That trip is going to be awesome,"* thought Coco Shantrel Dubois as she daydreamed a little longer.

9

AWESOME PHILANTHROPIST – SONNET 14

by
Sheryl Tillis

Hey, awesome philanthropist; great's your fate!

The welfare of others means so, so much,

In all that you'll do to participate,

Like paying it forward for such and such.

Charity is the focus of your life.

…Donating to one freely is your part;

Once it's fulfilled, love banishes ol' strife.

This may start with sowing seeds a la carte.

And yet, to form a team, we all must band.

Beauty is fine, but it's truly skin deep.

It doesn't matter if their house is tan.

…Generosity atones, then will seep.

Agape love lingers from day to day;

It is the rewards of God that will pay.

References

www.thespruceeats.com>... Top to Favorite
British Foods and Drinks-The Spruce Eats

Taste of Home.com/collection/
traditional-greek-food/

www.tasteatlas.com>50most-popular-
dishes-in-sicily

africanqueen.wordpress.com/2015/11/24/
thanksgiving-dinner-nigerian style

tasty.co>classic-nigerians-recipes-for-
beginners-jollof

16 Nigerian Recipes Every Needs to Try-Tasty

Niagara Escarpment Wikipedia

en.m.wikipedia.org>wiki>Niagara…

www.islands.com>carribbean-food-10-best-dishes-trin

http://cft.vanderbilt.edu>bloomstaxonomy

Blooms Taxonomy

http:www.histarch.illinois.edu>Ga…

Servants and Masters in the Plymouth Colony

Thanksgiving (United States) – wiki http:// en.m.wikipedia> wiki

KJV Super Giant Print Reference Bible; 1996 by Holman Bible Publishers; Matthews 7:12; the Golden Rule pg. 1463

CPSIA information can be obtained
at www.ICGtesting.com
Printed in the USA
LVHW092330150921
697901LV00002B/89